STEPPING STONE STORIES

Sue Lee's New Neighborhood
by Dr. Lawrence Balter

ADJUSTING TO A NEW HOME

Illustrated by Roz Schanzer

BARRON'S

New York • London • Toronto • Sydney

All inquiries should be addressed to:
Barron's Educational Series, Inc.
250 Wireless Boulevard
Hauppauge, NY 11788

International Standard Book No. 0-8120-6116-0

Library of Congress Catalog No. 89-6652

Library of Congress Cataloging-in-Publication Data

Balter, Lawrence.
Sue Lee's new neighborhood: adjusting to a new home/by
Lawrence Balter; illustrated by Roz Schanzer.
p. cm. (Stepping stone stories.)
Summary: A little girl faces the anxieties of moving, trading old
friends and familiar places for unfamiliar rooms and a new neigh-
borhood.
ISBN 0-8120-6116-0
[1. Moving, Household—Fiction.] I. Schanzer, Rosalyn, ill. II.
Title. III. Series.
PZ7.B2139Su 1989
[E]—dc19   89-6652
                                             CIP
                                             AC

PRINTED IN HONG KONG

9012   4900   987654321

Dear Parents and Teachers:

The books in this series were written to help young children better understand their own feelings and the feelings of others. It is hoped that by hearing these stories, or by reading them, children will see that they are not alone with their worries. They should also learn that there are constructive ways to deal with potentially disrupting circumstances.

All too often children's feelings are brushed aside by adults. Sometimes, because we want to protect youngsters and keep them happy, we inadvertently trivialize their concerns. But it is essential that we identify their emotions and understand their concerns before setting out to change things.

Children, of course, are more likely to act on their feelings than to reflect on them. After all, reflection requires tolerance that, in turn, calls for a degree of maturity. A first step, however, is learning to label and to talk about one's feelings.

I also hope to convey to parents and others who care for children that while some of a child's reactions may be troublesome, in all likelihood they are the normal by-products of some difficult situation with which the child is trying to cope. This is why children deserve our loving and patient guidance during their often painful and confusing journey toward adulthood.

Obviously, books can do only so much toward promoting self-understanding and problem-solving. I hope these stories will provide at least a helpful point of departure.

Lawrence Balter, Ph.D.

Very early on a Tuesday morning not too terribly
long ago in the town of Crescent Canyon
the sun was just coming up.

Sue Lee was the first one awake in her house.
Actually, she had not slept very well.
Strange dreams woke her during the night.
Then all the strange noises kept her awake.
And now she could not fall back to sleep.
The sun was just coming up and she could hear
birds chirping outside her window and squirrels
scurrying on the roof.

Sue Lee was not used to the sounds.
She looked around her room.
"I don't like these walls," she said. "They smell! It's ugly here."
A big tear rolled down her cheek.
"I just want to go back home," she said.

She slowly got up out of bed.
On her way across the room she stubbed her toe
on a box.
"Nothing is where it's supposed to be," she sobbed.
Then Sue Lee began to cry.
Her mother came in to see what was wrong.

"Oh dear, I'll bet you didn't sleep a wink last night," said her mother. "You look so tired and sad."
Sue Lee just looked down.
"I think you need a big hug!" her mother said. "Maybe that will cheer you up."

"No!" protested Sue Lee.
"What's the matter?" asked her mother.
"I hate it here," Sue Lee blurted out.
"What's wrong with it?" her mother asked.

"New house, new walls, smelly paint. New this! New that!" Sue Lee complained. "Why did we have to move anyway?"

"You know. We talked about that before. There's lots more space here for everybody," her mother reminded her. "You have a larger room. And it's closer to Dad's work."

"So what!" said Sue Lee.

"Come and look out the window. You liked this house when you saw that we could grow flowers over there and a vegetable garden there," her mother said.
Sue Lee turned away grumpily.
"And you even have your own swing set. Remember how excited you were when the family who used to live here said they'd leave it for you?" her mother said.

"Where are they now?" asked Sue Lee.
"They moved to a new house in another town," her mother said. "I wonder if the girl who lived here likes her new home."
"She doesn't! She wants to come back here to this house," Sue Lee answered. "And I wish she would. Then we could go back home."

"We can't go back there to live, but we can visit sometime," Sue Lee's mother suggested.

"Today!" shouted Sue Lee.

"We won't be able to go there today because we have a lot of chores to do here," her mother said. "Come on downstairs for a quick breakfast. We can try out the new kitchen together. Then we can go into town to do some shopping and exploring."

After she was dressed, Sue Lee walked downstairs on tiptoe so she wouldn't wake her dad.

"Look in that box over there for the toaster, and I'll get some dishes for us," said her mother.

"I want my blue cup," demanded Sue Lee.

"Well, it just so happens that I put it right here next to the plates so I'd know exactly where to find it when you asked," her mother said cheerfully.

Sue Lee did not feel very much like eating.

After a few nibbles of toast and a gulp of juice, she was ready for a walk around their new town.

The first store they came to was a delicatessen.
It had just opened.
"Let's go in and get some rolls for Dad's breakfast,"
her mother suggested.
The smells reminded Sue Lee of the deli in the
neighborhood she and her family had just moved
away from.
"I remember Mrs. Dee at our old deli," said Sue Lee.
"She always came out from behind the counter and
gave us a slice of cheese."
"Good morning," said the man in the store. "What can
I do for you?"
Sue Lee's mother bought some rolls, and on their way
out the man gave Sue Lee a tiny cracker that was
shaped like a fish.

"Next stop is the hardware store," her mother announced.
"We can buy a few packets of seeds for your gardens."
Inside the store, Sue Lee picked out seeds to grow green peppers, tomatoes, and leafy lettuce.
"I want these," she said.
Then she chose daisies, marigolds, and an envelope with a pretty purple flower on it.

"There's the library. And over there is the post office,"
her mother said. "And here's a store I hope is open."
"Not yet," said Sue Lee, noticing the locked door.
"Let's look in the window anyway," said her mother.
"Later, when it opens, you can choose some new
sheets and pillow cases for your bed and pick out
some special decorations for your room."

Sue Lee pointed out a rubber frog in the window.
"I'll bet that reminds you of our old next door
neighbor, Mr. Curtis, and his frogs," her mother said.
"He had a whole house full of frogs. But his were
glass and we couldn't even touch them. And they
couldn't hop or croak or anything," said Sue Lee.
And they laughed together about the funny man with
the frog collection who used to live next door.

"And then I had to move here," Sue Lee said unhappily.

"It will take some getting used to," said her mother.

"But I don't know anyone here. And it's so different," Sue Lee said sadly.

"It takes time. You don't have to cheer up right away, either," her mother continued. "After a while you'll make some new friends."

"But I liked it there," said Sue Lee.

"Once you get to know the neighborhood, it won't seem so different to you. Later, we'll walk over to the park and see if we can make some friends," suggested her mother.

When they arrived home, Dad was already dressed
for work and in the kitchen.
"We got some rolls for you at the new deli," said Sue Lee.
"Great. That's just what I'm in the mood for this
morning," her father said. "And then I have to get to
the office."

After breakfast they went out to the front porch and waved good-bye to her father as he drove off.

"Hi! Beautiful morning, isn't it?" said a woman walking toward their porch.

"Yes. It certainly is," answered Sue Lee's mother.

"I'm Marge Adams. This is my daughter Sandy. And her best friend Jessie is here for a visit. We live in the tan house across the way," she said. "I wanted to meet you, and the girls wanted to meet your daughter. And I thought you might like these strawberries from my backyard."

"I'm May Lin. And this is Sue Lee," said her mother.
"Thanks for the lovely berries. Would you like to come
in for a visit? Perhaps you kids would like to see
Sue Lee's room?"
Jessie and Sandy giggled.
"I'd love to," Sandy's mother said. "And I should
explain something. They know the house pretty
well. You see, Jessie used to live here."

"I know you," said Jessie.
"You do?" said Sue Lee with surprise.
"I saw you when you came to look at our house,"
Jessie said.
"But you didn't see Jessie because she always sat
outside on the swings," said Sandy.
"Why?" asked Sue Lee.
"She didn't want to talk to anyone," said Sandy.
"I didn't want anybody to buy my house," Jessie
explained. "Because I didn't want to move."

"I'm sorry we bought it," said Sue Lee. "Then we could have stayed home, too."

"It's not so bad now. Sandy came over to visit last week," Jessie said. "I got a little used to it."

"Which is your room?" asked Sandy. "The yellow one or the white one with the round rug? Can we go up and see?"

They dashed up the stairs together.

"Oh, now it's blue. It looks good this way," Jessie said.
"My bed used to be over there."
"You can see my room from your window," said
Sandy. "Do you have a flashlight?"
"In that box, I think. Why?" Sue Lee asked.
"Can I tell?" Jessie asked.
"Okay, but you have to whisper," said Sandy.
"Because we used to wait until it was really late. We
were supposed to be in bed," Jessie whispered. "And
then we got up and made signals with our flashlights.
No one even knew we were awake!"

"Sandy! Jessie! Come on down," called Mrs. Adams. "We have some marketing to do if you want some treats for dinner."

"Thanks for dropping by to welcome us," said Sue Lee's mother. "I hope we can get together again."

"I know the girls will never get to sleep tonight," said Sandy's mother. "Whenever they have a sleep-over they just talk and play all night long."

"Bye, Sue Lee," said Sandy and Jessie at the same time.

That afternoon Sue Lee and her mother bought some new pillow cases and sheets, but they did not have time to get to the park.

They spent the rest of the afternoon unpacking and decorating Sue Lee's room.

At dinner, Sue Lee told her father about the girl across the way and her friend who had lived in this house before.

Later, Sue Lee's mother kissed her good night.
"It's dark and pretty late. Sweet dreams," she said.
Then her father tucked her in for the night.
"I hope you're able to sleep well tonight," he said.

Sue Lee was tired, but she could not fall asleep.
It was still too new and different.
She began to think about her old school and some of
the kids she knew there.
Then she saw it.

A big yellow beam of light came shining through the
window and into her room.
Then came another one.
They swirled around on her walls.
She sat up in bed and her heart began to pound.

Suddenly, she realized that it was Jessie and Sandy talking to her with their flashlights.
Sue Lee searched quickly through the boxes until she found her flashlight.
Then she began to signal back to her new friends across the way.

Sue Lee stayed up really late that night.
She did not care if she would be tired tomorrow.
She had made her first new friends today.

It was dark, the stars were sparkling, and the sky was filled with dancing beams of warm yellow light.
It had turned out to be a pretty wonderful night in Crescent Canyon, after all!

About This Book

This story is about a child whose family has moved to a new community. Obviously, leaving one home for another is more than merely transferring body and belongings from one place to another. Relocating requires a great deal of preparation and adjustment for both children and parents.

Children need to be informed about your decision to move. The information should come from you, not some outside source, and the timing is critical. If you discuss it too far in advance, the tension can be very unsettling. Try to wait until you are certain that you will be relocating.

As obvious as it may seem to you, it is nevertheless important to reassure your children that they, too, are moving to the new place. Some children actually worry that they will be left behind when you go.

When they first hear the news of their upcoming relocation, many children voice objections. Their complaints should be listened to and respected. Parents very often feel anxious when their children do not show enthusiasm about the upcoming change. They are inclined to try to convince their children that all is for the best. But trying to talk your children out of their reactions is usually not very productive. Remember, children are very literal and, therefore, cannot mentally adjust to the new environment until they are actually in it.

When you actively begin to look for a new apartment or house, even young children can be included some of the time. As you narrow down your choices, bring the children along to see the ones you think might be finalists. Be certain to let them know that their possessions will replace the ones that are presently in the house, and that its occupants and furniture will be going somewhere else.

When the packing begins, children should be encouraged to fill a few cartons, too. It will make them feel part of the process and also enable them to find some of their favorite things when they get to the new house. In fact, for the same reason, it is wise to carry some special things personally rather than send them in the moving van.

On moving day, do not send the children off with a baby-sitter for the entire time. If possible, allow them to see aspects of the beginning, middle, and end of the moving process. Young children can also be encouraged to play moving games. They can pack some items and cart them from one room to another in order to master the concept of relocation.

Expect some initial reactions after you have moved to a new home and neighborhood. Sleeplessness is not uncommon, and a finicky eater may be a little more so during this stressful time. Don't be surprised by some clinginess on the part of an otherwise independent youngster. If handled properly, however, the adjustment period for young children should not exceed a few months.

In this story, Sue Lee and her family have just spent their first night in their new home. Although she had been prepared for the move, Sue Lee is not very pleased. Now is when her adjustment must begin. In addition to offering her emotional comfort, Sue Lee's mother introduces a series of constructive activities to help Sue Lee cope with her apprehensions. Then, the unexpected arrival of children her own age, along with an unusual nighttime encounter, set the stage for Sue Lee's first satisfying steps in the process of becoming comfortable in her new environment. I hope this story will provide insights and strategies that can make a change in your living arrangements a positive adventure for you and your children.